The Pain of Progression

By: Apostle Dr. Robert L. Black

Apostle Dr. Robert L. Black

Copyright © 2026

All Rights Reserved

ISBN: 978-1-964365-91-6

The Times Publishers

Dedication

To the warriors of silent battles.

This book is for you — for the bruised, the tired, the determined. May you see your suffering not as a setback, but as the birthplace of your evolution.

"Resilience is the quiet faith that, though we walk through valleys, we are never without the strength God places within us. For every trial shapes us, just as endurance has been promised to work patience in us."

— Inspired by James 1:2–4

Table of Contents

Author's Acknowledgment

From Apostle Dr. Robert Black

"The Pain of Progression"

My deepest gratitude begins at home. To my beloved wife, Lady Stacey Black, and entire family—your unwavering love, patience, and strength have carried me through every chapter of this journey. You have stood beside me during moments of stretching, breaking, healing, and rebuilding. Your faith in me has been an anchor when the weight of calling felt heavy, and the road of purpose felt long. I honor you, and I thank God for the gift of each of you.

To my spiritual sons and daughters, brothers and sisters in the faith, Divine Alignment Kingdom Association, Total Worship Center, and every covenant connection God has assigned to my life—thank you for your prayers, encouragement, and belief in the oil upon my life. Ministry is not walked alone, and I am grateful for every hand that has helped me build, every voice that has spoken life, and every heart that has sown into this vision.

A special acknowledgment is dedicated to every reader who feels caught between where you are and where God is calling you—the place I call "The Middle."

The Middle is where pressure meets purpose, where pain pushes you toward promise, and where progression doesn't always look or feel like movement. This book is for those who are wrestling with the tension of becoming; those who feel stretched, stuck, or suspended between process and destiny. You are not forgotten, and you are not failing—you are simply in transition.

May these pages remind you that your pain is not punishment; it is preparation. Your process is not accidental; it is intentional. And your Middle is not a stopping point; it is a shaping place.

Finally, to God—my source, my strength, and the author of my purpose. Every revelation, every testimony, every victory, and every challenge that birthed this book belongs to You. Thank You for trusting me with the assignment.

With gratitude and grace,

Apostle Dr. Robert Black.

Foreword by Bishop Steven Hutchinson

There is a season most believers intimately know, but few know how to articulately name and explain. It is the season where heaven has spoken a promise, but earth has not yet seen its production. It's after the calling, but before you receive clarity of what's next. I've labeled it "the until season." But Apostle Black eloquently labels it: "the middle."

The Pain of Progression speaks directly to those moments when life feels slow, and you're questioning if you're behind. With pastoral sensitivity and spiritual depth, Apostle Dr. Robert Black guides the reader through the uncomfortable truth that growth often hurts; not because you did something wrong, but because you need to develop. When God is forming, sometimes that process can feel unfavorable.

That's what I appreciate most about this work is its refusal to romanticize progression. This book acknowledges the grief, the frustration, the questions, and the silent nights that accompany becoming. While at the same time, it never leaves the reader without hope. It reframes pain as purposeful, delay as developmental, and valleys as divine classrooms.

This book will resonate with anyone who has ever asked God, "Where are you? Why does it have to be this way?" And gently, faithfully, it responds: "Because you are being prepared for more."

As you read, my prayer is that you stop pressuring or rushing yourself. That you will stop measuring your life by speed instead of obedience. That, although you may not see any visible fruit, God is strengthening and deepening your roots, so that this is the root season of your life.

Welcome to the middle!

This is not where your story ends. This is where your story is made.

Acknowledgement by Pastor J.J. Miles

The Pain of Progression by Apostle Dr. Robert L. Black

When I think of Apostle Dr. Robert L. Black, I think of a man who is truly sold out for God, fully committed to doing the will of the Father. He is loyal, honorable, trustworthy, kind, consistent, and a man of integrity who carries a spirit of excellence in all that he does. Beyond ministry, he is a devoted family man—a loving husband, an amazing father, a faithful son and brother, a wonderful uncle, and a trusted friend. He understands that true leadership begins at home and flows outward. His life reflects not only a deep devotion to God's call but a sincere commitment to stewarding well every relationship God has entrusted to him.

I have known him in many roles—as Brother Black, Pastor Black, Uncle Rob, and my friend—and in every season, he has proven himself worthy of trust. I trust him as a man who sincerely seeks the Lord and faithfully hears His voice. His perspective has been of great value to me throughout my own journey—growing up in church, stepping into ministry, and now serving as a pastor in the Lord's Church. His wisdom, consistency, and spiritual insight have been a steady presence along the way.

What resonated with me most in The Pain of Progression is the revelation that the "middle" is where identity is forged and purpose is clarified. This book powerfully highlights the importance of enduring the process, because there are some things that can only be shaped, refined, and fully understood in the middle season. Purpose is not merely discovered at the end—it is formed along the way.

As a pastor, I have seen far too many people rush toward outcomes without understanding the importance of preparation. The waiting seasons—though uncomfortable— are often where God is doing His deepest work. Pain and delay are not always punishment; many times, they are protection. I have witnessed this truth in ministry and in the lives of people navigating careers, marriages, the desire for family, and the call to trust God's timing even when it feels like nothing is moving. Those who remain focused on trusting God ultimately discover that His divine will is always best.

This message also testifies to my own life's journey in leadership, ministry, and calling. There have been many seasons where it felt as though God had me on the back side of the mountain—close enough to learn what to do and what not to do, yet hidden enough to be shaped. Even in painful moments, when it seemed as though God had forgotten what He spoke concerning me, He was still causing me to progress. Those seasons taught me to trust Him, hold fast to His Word, protect my integrity, and allow my character to be shaped so I could steward well everything He placed in my hands—knowing it all belongs to God and not to me.

This book is especially needed in this season. We live in a time where few want to endure the process. Everything is expected to be quick, painless, and convenient. Yet it is through progression—often through pain—that character is built. Growth requires separation, and maturity demands endurance.

While this book will undoubtedly bless leaders both inside and outside the Church, it is also for anyone who refuses to give up and desires more out of life. If you carry big dreams—not just for yourself, but to bless others—this book is for you.

I am deeply grateful for this contribution to the Body of Christ and to every reader who will encounter these pages. Growth may be painful because it requires separation, but valleys are not curses—they are classrooms. Pain does not mean you missed God; often, it means you obeyed Him. The middle is where identity is forged, and purpose is clarified. As Scripture reminds us, all things work together for good to those who love God and are called according to His purpose (Romans 8:28). God has never wasted a tear, a delay, or a season of pressure.

Trust His Process.

Pastor J.J. Mills.

Excerpt: The Pain of Progression

I believe many in the Body of Christ today find themselves "in the middle," unsure whether they are missing the mark concerning their ultimate purpose. The middle often feels uncomfortable, stagnant, and even like a hindrance to progress. Yet, paradoxically, the middle is where strength is built, balance is developed, and identity is clarified.

Consider the life of David — from outcast to shepherd boy, to ultimately becoming King over all Israel (1 Samuel 16 through 2 Samuel 5). David's *middle* was the valley, or what I call *his Vast Valley Experiential Experience.*

It was in the vastness of that valley that David learned how to defeat lions and bears that crossed his path. It was in the middle that David became a giant slayer, conquering Goliath. David's confidence came from knowing exactly who his enemies were — and more importantly, who his God was. His bold declaration echoed from the depths of revelation: *"Who is this uncircumcised Philistine, that he should defy the armies of the living God?"*

Though David endured approximately thirteen years in his valley season, he understood he was right where God needed him to be. He was "in the middle" — yet fully aligned with purpose. Because God was with him, he could not be defeated.

Our ultimate example is Jesus the Christ. In the middle of His divine assignment as Savior of the world, Jesus encountered His own "middle" at Calvary. It was there He suffered, endured the cross, and despised the shame — yet remained anchored in purpose.

This book, *The Pain of Progression*, is written for those who feel stuck "in the middle" — those being processed, refined, and prepared for the fullness of their calling. I want you to know: **God is with you, and He never fails.**

The Pain of Progression calls the believer to move beyond simply completing tasks or following steps — the mechanics we call *process*. Instead, it challenges you to focus on the deeper meaning behind the process: your *purpose*. It is an invitation to see the larger vision rather than just the instructions.

Two Sample Action Points & Key Takeaways

1. Process through Progression provides structure, but embracing the pain within purpose gives freedom.

Progression provides structure that produces consistent results, but embracing the pain tied to purpose grants mental flexibility and spiritual freedom. When you understand the "why," you can properly balance the process — and confidently reach the end God intended.

Romans 8:28 *"And we know..."* ("know" implies relational experience — the lessons formed in the middle of both the good and the arduous). *"...that all things work together for good to those who love God, to those who are called according to His purpose."*

2. Affliction carries goodness when viewed through God's lens.

The goodness of affliction equips you to navigate your valley both mentally and spiritually. Relationship with God secures a hope that your natural eyes cannot see.

Psalm 119:71 *"It is good for me that I have been afflicted, that I might learn thy statutes."*

Introduction — When Purpose Meets Process

Every journey with God has a beginning and an end—but it is the middle that forms us. The middle is where purpose collides with process, where the promise God spoke meets the reality of who we must become to carry it. It is the space between prophecy and fulfillment—an often uncomfortable stretch where faith is refined, character is strengthened, and trust is tested.

We celebrate mountaintop moments. We testify when doors open, when prayers are answered, when direction becomes clear. But we rarely speak with the same enthusiasm about the valleys—the detours, delays, disappointments, and silent seasons that sit between obedience and outcome. Yet it is in those in-between places that God does His deepest work.

The middle exposes what the mountaintop cannot. It reveals fear that still lingers, pride that still competes, and attachments that cannot accompany us into our next season. It teaches us that progression is not always visible and rarely glamorous. Sometimes growth feels like resistance. Sometimes obedience feels costly. Sometimes faith feels stretched thin.

Progression hurts because growth requires separation. We cannot step fully into what will be while clinging to what was. Throughout Scripture, those called by God were shaped in this tension. Joseph had a dream, but he also had a pit. David was anointed, but he also endured the wilderness. Paul carried revelation, yet wrestled with a thorn. Even Jesus embraced Gethsemane before the resurrection. Pain was never proof of abandonment; it was preparation for assignment.

God does not allow valleys to break His people, but to build them. He does not permit pressure to punish, but to prepare. The valley is not evidence that you missed God—it is often confirmation that you are becoming who He intended you to be. The middle becomes a sacred classroom where trust deepens beyond emotion, understanding, and personal timelines.

This book was born out of my own middle. I have known seasons where obedience cost more than expected and where progress felt indistinguishable from pain. I have walked through transitions that were both blessings and breakups. Yet in hindsight, I see God's fingerprints in every delay, every closed door, every uncomfortable stretch. None of it was wasted. It was shaping me—forming a capacity I did not know I possessed, but God always intended.

The Pain of Progression is more than a concept. It is a lived reality. And perhaps, it is yours as well.

My prayer is that as you read, you begin to reinterpret your middle. That you recognize God is not merely moving you forward—He is growing you upward. That you understand pressure has purpose, pruning has intention, and pain carries prophecy.

If you feel stalled, unseen, or uncertain, hear this clearly:

You are not stuck.

You are not behind.

You are not forgotten.

You are being formed.

You are progressing—step by step, stretch by stretch, valley by valley.

Welcome to the middle.

Welcome to the making.

Welcome to the process that leads to purpose.

Chapter Outlines — The Pain of Progression

Chapter 1: The Challenge of Progression

Focus: Understanding why growth is uncomfortable and why God allows seasons of stretching.

Sections:

1. **The Myth of Easy Elevation**
   Why spiritual promotion requires spiritual pressure.
2. **When God Calls You Forward, but Life Pulls You Back**
   The tension between calling and current circumstances.
3. **David's Early Challenges**
   From oil to obscurity: Anointing doesn't eliminate difficulty.
4. **Why the Middle Feels Like Resistance**
   Progression requires friction.

Takeaways: How to recognize God's hand in difficult transitions?

Chapter 2: Joy Speaks Louder Than Pain

Focus: Learning how divine joy becomes strength during suffering.

Sections:

5. **Happiness vs. Joy**

   The difference between emotional relief and spiritual strength.

6. **Joy as a Weapon**

   How praise silences the enemy.

7. **David's Praise in the Valley**

   Worship as survival.

8. **Maintaining Joy When Nothing Changes**

   Faith that shouts from the middle.

Takeaways: Tools to activate joy in pain.

Chapter 3: The Intimacy of Persistency

Focus: How consistency creates intimacy with God.

Sections:

9. **Persistence Builds Proximity**

   How continual pursuit draws you closer to God.

10. David's Discipline in Isolation

Worship, warfare, and waiting in the shepherd's field.

11. When Silence Feels Personal

Understanding God's quiet seasons.

12. The Spiritual Reward of Showing Up Daily

Progression is built on persistence.

Takeaways: Habits that cultivate spiritual stamina.

Chapter 4: The Roadblocks of Pursuit

Focus: Recognizing and overcoming obstacles to purpose.

Sections:

13. Internal Roadblocks

Doubt, fear, insecurity, self-sabotage.

14. External Roadblocks

People, systems, environments, spiritual warfare.

15. David's Roadblocks

Family rejection, Saul's persecution, and misunderstanding.

16. How God Uses Roadblocks as Redirection

Delays as divine detours.

Takeaways: Strategies for breakthrough.

Chapter 5: The Damage of Anxiousness

Focus: How anxiety disrupts spiritual alignment.

Sections:

17. Anxiety: The Enemy of Focus

18. Fear of Failure vs. Fear of Success

19. David's Emotional Turmoil in the Wilderness

20. What Anxiety Teaches Us About Trust

Anxiety reveals where faith must grow.

Takeaways: How to spiritually manage anxiety in the middle.

Chapter 6: Purpose Is Passionate

Focus: Discovering the fire behind your assignment.

Sections:

21. Purpose Requires Heart, Not Just Skill

22. How Pain Awakens Passion

23. David's Passion for God, God's People, and God's Presence

24. The Cost of Purpose

Passion will challenge your comfort.

Takeaways: Identifying and activating God-given passion.

Chapter 7: Living the Outcome in Full View

Focus: How to see the finish while standing in the middle.

Sections:

25. The Power of Vision

Seeing spiritually what hasn't manifested naturally.

26. David's Glimpse of Kingship

27. The Danger of Living Without Sight

28. Developing a Faith-Filled Future Focus

Takeaways: Visualizing your victory before it arrives.

Chapter 8: P.A.I.N. — Positional, Agreement, Identifying, Normalcy

Focus: A revelatory breakdown of what pain teaches and produces.

Sections:

29. P – Positional

Pain positions you for purpose.

30. A – Agreement

Coming into agreement with God's process.

31. I – Identifying

Recognizing who you are and who your enemy is.

32. N – Normalcy

Making maturity your new normal.

Takeaways: How P.A.I.N. becomes your teacher, not your tormentor.

Chapter 9: Failure Is Never an Option When Faith Embraces Progression

Focus: Understanding why believers cannot fail when aligned with God.

Sections:

33. The Myth of Failure in God

34. Faith as a Stabilizer

35. David's "Failures" That Built Him

36. How Progression Guarantees Victory

Every setback advances maturity.

Takeaways: Learning to redefine failure through God's lens.

Chapter 10: The Restoration in the Valley

Focus: How God restores strength, identity, and purpose in valley seasons.

Sections:

37. The Valley as a Refining Place

38. God's Restoration Process

39. David's Rise After the Valley

40. Why Restoration Is Required Before Promotion

Takeaways: Expectation for God's restoration in your middle.

Conclusion — Purpose Prevails

Focus: Encouragement, declaration, and final prophetic push.

Sections:

41. Summarizing the message of the middle.

42. Calling the reader into spiritual maturity.

43. Pronouncing breakthrough and progression.

44. Final encouragement: God never wastes pain.

CHAPTER 1

THE CHALLENGE OF PROGRESSION

From **The Pain of Progression** *by Apostle Dr. Robert L. Black (All Scripture: NKJV)*

Progression is not gentle. It rarely feels comfortable, and it does not promise convenience. More often than not, it arrives as a disruption. It calls you forward while simultaneously confronting what must be healed, refined, or surrendered within you. What feels like instability is often an invitation.

Every believer who longs to walk in purpose will eventually encounter the demands of growth. Not because God intends harm, but because destiny carries weight. The future God designed for you requires a capacity that cannot be formed in ease. Growth requires resistance. Purpose requires pressure. Elevation requires endurance.

This is where many misunderstand the journey. We celebrate the oil of anointing but overlook the obscurity that often follows it. We rejoice in the promise yet resist the process that prepares us to carry it. We desire the throne without the valley, the crown without the crushing, the assignment without the agitation that strengthens our character.

Yet Scripture consistently reveals a pattern: calling is followed by challenge. Anointing is followed by development. No prophet, king, disciple, or believer stepped into destiny without first being shaped by difficulty.

When God Calls You Forward, but Life Pulls You Back

One of the greatest tensions of progression is this: God speaks advancement while your environment reflects limitation.

He calls you forward while your circumstances resemble your past.

He calls you more while life still labels you less.

He calls you chosen while others see you as ordinary.

He calls you anointed while situations suggest inadequacy.

He calls you destined while seasons feel delayed.

This tension can feel contradictory, but it is not punishment—it is preparation.

What appears to be a setback is often structural reinforcement. God strengthens foundations before He builds higher levels. He deepens roots before He extends branches. Like an archer pulling back a bow, what feels like retreat is often stored momentum.

Progression rarely appears as an obvious advancement. At times, it resembles reduction. At times, it feels like a decline. At times, it seems as though everything is moving in reverse.

But in God, backward is not regression—it is alignment. It is positioning. It is a strategy unfolding beyond your immediate perspective.

David understood this tension.

David: The Anointed Yet Unprepared

When Samuel anointed David in 1 Samuel 16, destiny touched his head—but process still governed his steps. The oil flowed, yet elevation did not immediately follow. He was anointed before his brothers, affirmed in private, and then sent back to the fields.

The anointing did not escort him to a palace.

It returned him to a pasture.

Why?

Because calling without capacity is dangerous, promotion without preparation is unstable. The challenge of progression demanded development.

David carried the calling, but not yet the capacity.

He bore the anointing, but not yet the experience.

He had favor, but not yet the foundation.

Before he confronted Goliath publicly, he had to defeat lions and bears privately. Before he led a nation, he had to lead himself. Before he could steward influence, he had to steward isolation.

This is the pattern of progression: God reveals the end, but begins with formation.

David's story confronts a truth many resist—there is always a middle between calling and crowning. Between promise and fulfillment lies preparation. And it is in that middle place that God shapes what the promise requires.

Why the Middle Feels Like Resistance

The middle often feels like opposition, but resistance is not evidence of abandonment. It is one of God's primary tools for strengthening what He intends to elevate.

The middle feels difficult because a transformation is occurring.

You are outgrowing former identities.

You are stretching into a larger assignment.

You are releasing habits and mindsets that cannot accompany you forward.

You are learning a deeper submission.

You are being refined for greater responsibility.

Resistance signals development.

The mountaintop may display victory, but the valley builds capacity. The wilderness sharpens discernment. The in-between deepens obedience. In hidden seasons, God addresses the inner life—the unseen motivations, insecurities, and dependencies that would undermine public success.

Most importantly, resistance exposes what still resists God within you. The friction you feel is often the friction between who you were and who you are becoming.

The middle confronts what must end so something stronger can begin. It requires the death of former patterns so new maturity can live.

The Discomfort of Divine Development

Progression is uncomfortable because transformation rarely happens in ease. We do not mature in environments that protect our comfort—we mature in environments that challenge our assumptions, stretch our capacity, and confront our limitations.

Discomfort serves a purpose. It compels us to evaluate where we truly stand. It forces us to reconsider what we believe and why we believe it. It exposes fears we have managed to avoid and highlights areas we have neglected. It stretches us beyond familiar boundaries and presses us into deeper trust.

Through discomfort, God reshapes dependency.

Pain begins to instruct.

Pressure begins to strengthen.

Uncertainty begins to clarify.

What initially feels disruptive often becomes directional. Discomfort redirects our reliance from self-sufficiency to spiritual surrender.

If the middle were painless, we would remain there. If it required nothing of us, we would never grow beyond it. But purpose demands expansion—and expansion requires stretching.

Discomfort is not the enemy of destiny; it is often its doorway.

When Progress Doesn't Look Like Progress

One of the most challenging aspects of spiritual growth is that progression rarely appears obvious. You may be advancing without visible evidence. You may be developing while feeling delayed.

Progression often hides beneath circumstances that seem contradictory:

Delays that test patience.

Opposition that strengthens conviction.

Confusion that sharpens discernment.

Spiritual warfare that deepens prayer.

Loneliness that intensifies intimacy with God.

Seasons of waiting that cultivate endurance.

Being overlooked builds humility.

Being underestimated that refines confidence.

Starting over that strengthens resilience.

Closed doors that redirect your steps.

What appears stagnant may actually be strategic.

Progression is not merely forward movement—it is forward formation. God is shaping your spirit, expanding your stamina, refining your character, and stabilizing your faith. These changes often occur beneath the surface, unseen but substantial.

The absence of visible results does not mean the absence of divine activity. Growth can be silent. Development can be hidden. Formation can be slow.

But unseen does not mean unproductive.

You Are Growing Even When You Feel Stuck

David did not recognize, in the moment, that the pasture was preparing him for battle. While tending sheep, he was developing courage. While running from Saul, he was cultivating resilience. While hiding in caves, he was learning leadership under pressure.

The preparation did not resemble promotion, but it was essential to it.

You will not always recognize growth while it is happening. Development is often subtle. Maturity forms gradually. Strength increases quietly. What feels like stagnation may actually be stabilization.

You may not see what is changing within you—but God does.

One of the challenges of progression is that God builds in obscurity before He elevates in visibility. Public influence is sustained by private formation. Victory in front of others is secured in hidden places. The integrity no one applauds becomes the foundation everyone benefits from later.

Your private struggles are constructing public stability.

Your unseen obedience is preparing visible responsibility.

Your hidden sacrifices are strengthening your future assignment.

Nothing surrendered in the middle is wasted.

The Grace to Endure the Middle

If these words resonate with you, it is likely because you are standing in the space between where you were and where God is leading you. The middle can feel uncertain. It can feel stretched and unfamiliar. It can feel slower than expected.

But the middle is not a mistake.

It is not failure—it is formation.

It is not rejection—it is refinement.

It is not a delay—it is development.

The middle is where strength aligns with purpose. It is where character catches up to calling. It is where God constructs what the promise will require.

If you feel stalled, you are not stuck—you are being shaped.

If you feel unseen, you are not forgotten—you are being refined.

If you feel delayed, you are not behind—you are being positioned.

If you feel pressured, you are not defeated—you are being developed.

Progression may involve discomfort, but it carries direction. It may involve pain, but it carries promise.

Every challenge you face in this season is preparing you for the responsibility you cannot yet fully see.

The throne may feel distant, but the preparation is present.

And the preparation is purposeful.

CHAPTER 2

JOY SPEAKS LOUDER THAN PAIN

*From **The Pain of Progression** by Apostle Dr. Robert L. Black (All Scripture: NKJV)*

Progression carries weight. With that weight comes pressure, discomfort, and at times an emotional intensity that is difficult to articulate. Growth stretches the inner life. Calling exposes vulnerability. Transition unsettles what once felt stable.

Pain has a voice—and it is not quiet.

It speaks through disappointment and delay. It echoes through betrayal and loss. It whispers in seasons where clarity fades, and outcomes remain uncertain. In the middle, pain can feel dominant. It demands attention. It questions identity. It attempts to redefine your narrative and mute your sense of purpose.

But pain is not the loudest voice available to you.

There is a greater voice—steady, anchored, and authoritative.

That voice is joy.

Joy is not the absence of pain; it is the presence of strength within it. It is not emotional excitement, nor is it denial of hardship. Joy is spiritual empowerment. It is a God-given resilience that stabilizes the soul when circumstances attempt to destabilize it.

"The joy of the Lord is your strength." — **Nehemiah 8:10**

Joy fortifies what pain attempts to fracture. It steadies what pressure tries to shake. It anchors what uncertainty threatens to uproot.

In seasons where pain raises its volume, joy answers with authority.

Happiness Reacts — Joy Remains

One of the most common misconceptions among believers is equating happiness with joy. Though related, they are not the same.

Happiness is circumstantial. Joy is covenantal.

Happiness is reactive. Joy is rooted.

Happiness rises and falls with events. Joy flows from a relationship.

Happiness depends on what happens around you.

Joy depends on what God has placed within you.

Happiness fluctuates.

Joy endures.

Happiness fades under pressure.

Joy strengthens under pressure.

Happiness requires favorable conditions.

Joy thrives on faithful expectation.

This distinction matters in seasons of progression. Happiness cannot sustain you in the valley. It cannot carry you through misunderstanding, delay, or spiritual testing. It cannot hold steady while God reshapes your character and reorders your priorities.

But joy can.

Joy quietly affirms, "God is still present."

Joy reassures, "This season has purpose."

Joy declares, "What feels like breaking is actually building."

Pain may speak loudly—but joy speaks from a deeper authority.

Joy does not deny hardship; it reinterprets it. It reminds you that the middle is not meaningless and that pressure does not cancel promise.

Joy as a Weapon of Warfare

Joy is often reduced to a feeling, but Scripture presents it as something far more powerful. Joy is not merely emotional—it is strategic. In spiritual warfare, not every battle is fought through confrontation. Some victories are secured through worship. Some breakthroughs are birthed through praise. Some strongholds are dismantled by a faith-filled refusal to surrender to despair.

Joy becomes a weapon when it refuses to bow to darkness.

It disrupts the enemy's strategy.

It confounds accusations and intimidation.

It interrupts cycles of discouragement.

It weakens the grip of despair.

It stabilizes the soul under attack.

The adversary expects collapse under pressure. Joy responds with confidence.

David understood this dimension of joy. His worship was not performance; it was preservation. His praise was not emotional excess; it was spiritual alignment. When life pressed him, he did not retreat inward—he turned upward.

When surrounded by enemies, he sang. When fear whispered uncertainty, he lifted his voice in declaration.

David's joy was not anchored to his circumstances; it was anchored to his covenant with God.

That is what made it unshakable.

David's Praise in the Valley

Before David ever governed a nation, he learned to govern himself. Before he ruled a kingdom, he learned to steward his inner world. The valley became his training ground—not only for leadership, but for emotional and spiritual maturity.

In obscurity, he cultivated devotion.

Without an audience, he developed consistency.

While overlooked, he strengthened intimacy.

In crisis, he "strengthened himself in the Lord" (1 Samuel 30:6).

Joy in the valley is not a loud celebration—it is disciplined trust.

It looks like praising when emotions resist.

It looks like rejoicing when circumstances feel unfair.

It looks like singing through tears.

It looks like trusting when answers are delayed.

It looks like lifting your hands when your heart feels heavy.

Joy does not wait for ideal conditions. It rises precisely where pain once dominated. It fills spaces where fear attempted to silence hope.

When pressure increases, joy becomes spiritual oxygen. It allows your faith to breathe when everything around you feels suffocating.

In the valley, joy is not optional—it is essential.

Joy Is a Revelation, Not a Reaction

Joy cannot be fabricated. It cannot be manufactured through effort or maintained through emotional discipline alone. Joy is not something you produce—it is something you receive.

Joy is born from revelation.

It emerges from knowing who God is, even when you cannot fully understand what He is doing. It flows from confidence in His character, not clarity about your circumstances.

Joy rests in truths that transcend visible outcomes.

It knows, "God is working, even while I am waiting."

It declares, "God is faithful, even when results remain unseen."

It believes, "My purpose is intact, even when my path is unclear."

Pain attempts to pull your focus backward—to what was lost, what failed, or what has not yet happened. Joy redirects your vision forward—to what God has promised and who He has always proven Himself to be.

Pain magnifies obstacles.

Joy magnifies God.

Pain insists the season is ending.

Joy insists the promise is alive.

When joy is rooted in revelation, the middle no longer feels meaningless. It becomes strategic. What once felt like suffering begins to reveal purpose. What once felt like an interruption begins to uncover intention.

Joy reframes the season.

Maintaining Joy When Nothing Changes

There are seasons in progression where visible movement slows. You pray, yet the response feels delayed. You serve faithfully, yet recognition does not come. You believe, yet circumstances remain unchanged.

It is in these moments that many lose spiritual momentum—not because God has withdrawn, but because they have surrendered their joy.

Joy is not sustained by visible progress. It thrives in hidden growth. It deepens in quiet seasons. It matures when outcomes are still forming.

Joy grows in the unseen.

It strengthens in the unchanging.

It develops in routine obedience.

It stabilizes during waiting.

Maintaining joy in such seasons requires intentional alignment.

First, anchor yourself in who God is. Joy is rooted in His character—unchanging, faithful, sovereign. When your understanding wavers, His nature does not.

Second, remember what He has already done. Testimonies build confidence. Past faithfulness becomes fuel for present endurance.

Third, remain connected to His presence. Joy flourishes where communion is prioritized. Worship, prayer, and Scripture recalibrate the heart.

Fourth, guard your internal environment. Joy cannot coexist with constant exposure to fear, cynicism, and negativity. What you continually consume shapes what you consistently feel.

Fifth, speak life intentionally. Words reinforce perspective. Declaring truth strengthens faith and steadies the soul.

Joy does not merely accompany faith—it sustains it. When faith grows weary, joy strengthens its resolve. When clarity fades, joy keeps confidence intact.

In seasons where nothing seems to change, joy reminds you that something is still forming.

When Joy Speaks Louder, Pain Loses Power

When joy is truly activated, something shifts internally. Circumstances may remain unchanged, but your posture toward them transforms.

Pain no longer defines your identity.

Fear loses its authority over your decisions.

Discouragement cannot dismantle your resolve.

Darkness cannot silence your faith.

Delay cannot cancel your destiny.

Joy does not remove pressure—it strengthens you within it. It enables you to outlast seasons that were designed to overwhelm you. It allows you to stand upright in moments that were meant to bend you. It stabilizes your spirit when everything around you feels unstable.

Joy does not deny the presence of pain—it overrides its dominance.

Pain may present facts.

Joy proclaims truth.

Pain says, "This is too much."

Joy responds, "You are being strengthened."

Pain whispers, "You will not recover."

Joy declares, "You will rise."

Pain suggests, "This season defines you."

Joy affirms, "This season is shaping you."

When joy speaks louder than pain, perspective shifts. What once felt like breaking begins to look like building. What once felt like an ending begins to resemble preparation.

And above every competing voice, joy anchors you in the greatest truth of all:

God is present.

God is faithful.

God does not fail.

That truth alone is enough to carry you through the middle.

CHAPTER 3

THE INTIMACY OF PERSISTENCY

*From **The Pain of Progression** by Apostle Dr. Robert L. Black (All Scripture: NKJV)*

Progression rewards those who refuse to release what God has spoken. Destiny is not carried by casual interest; it is sustained by consistent pursuit. What God entrusts deeply is rarely discovered through talent alone, but through disciplined devotion.

God's presence is not hidden from His people—it is revealed to those who keep returning. Those who revisit the altar. Those who reopen the Word. Those who return to prayer even when answers delay. Over time, proximity becomes intimacy, and intimacy produces transformation.

The Spirit is inviting believers into a deeper consistency—not empty repetition, but a holy rhythm. A cadence of worship, prayer, obedience, and surrender woven into daily life. Persistency is more than repeated activity; it is steady alignment. It is the choice to remain when enthusiasm fades, to pray when clarity is absent, to trust when evidence is limited.

It is not dramatic—but it is decisive.

"But let patience have its perfect work, that you may be perfect and complete, lacking nothing." — **James 1:4**

"Then you will call upon Me and go and pray to Me, and I will listen to you. And you will **seek Me and find Me, when you search for Me with all your heart.**" — **Jeremiah 29:12–13**

Persistency creates conditions where maturity can develop. It refines character under steady heat. It opens pathways into deeper communion with God. Those who remain are not rewarded because they pressure God, but because remaining reshapes them into vessels capable of carrying greater responsibility.

Persistence Builds Proximity

Intimacy with God is not built in isolated moments—it grows through repeated return. It is not sustained by intensity alone, but by consistency over time.

Those who return, receive.

Those who knock, enter.

Those who wait, are strengthened.

"But those who wait on the LORD shall renew their strength; they shall mount up with wings like eagles, they shall run and not be weary, they shall walk and not faint." — **Isaiah 40:31**

Waiting is not inactivity—it is anchored expectation. It is disciplined trust expressed daily. As you remain faithful in seeking God, proximity increases. And as proximity increases, clarity deepens, strength renews, and intimacy expands.

Persistency turns pursuit into a relationship. And a relationship becomes the foundation for lasting progression.

Prophetic Declaration — "The Intimacy of Persistency" *(NKJV Inspired)*

I decree and declare that **as you persist, heaven responds**.

I declare that every step you take toward God draws Him closer to you in power, revelation, and intimacy.

I declare that the Lord is strengthening your spirit with endurance,

your heart with unwavering devotion,

and your mind with supernatural focus.

I declare that every day you choose to seek Him,

your capacity increases,

your discernment sharpens,

your hunger grows,

and your identity becomes more defined in Him.

I decree that **the spirit of weariness breaks off your life now**.

Every assignment of distraction, discouragement, and delay is bound and cast down in Jesus' name.

I declare that your **daily pursuit is becoming a prophetic rhythm —**

a rhythm that draws the voice of God into your atmosphere,

the presence of God into your home,

and the glory of God into your future.

I prophesy that **your persistence is unlocking divine access**.

Visions will open.

Dreams will increase.

Clarity will return.

Strength will rise.

Faith will stabilize.

Purpose will ignite.

I decree that you will **not faint in the middle**.

You will not turn back.

You will not grow weary in well-doing.

You will not lose heart in the waiting.

For the Lord your God goes with you, before you, and within you.

I declare that a new mantle of **spiritual consistency** is resting upon you.

A fresh grace to pray.

A fresh grace to worship.

A fresh grace to obey.

A fresh grace to remain.

A fresh grace to endure.

I prophesy that your persistence is becoming **the birthplace of divine intimacy —**

where you will hear God differently,

see God differently,

and know God differently.

I decree that the next dimension of your destiny

will be revealed not by striving,

but by **remaining**.

And so I declare in Jesus' name:

You shall persist.

You shall progress.

You shall prevail.

And you shall walk in the fullness of intimacy with the living God. Amen.

CHAPTER 4

THE ROADBLOCKS OF PURSUIT

From **The Pain of Progression** *by Apostle Dr. Robert L. Black (All Scripture: NKJV)*

Progression always attracts resistance because destiny carries weight. The greater the purpose, the heavier the opposition. The enemy does not fight what lacks significance; he resists what threatens his territory. Roadblocks are not meant to end your journey—they are designed to reveal your stature in the Spirit and refine your readiness to carry what God has ordained.

In pursuit of purpose, there will be gates that must be approached, giants that must be confronted, and weights that must be laid aside. But in the midst of opposition, the Spirit's voice continually declares: "Keep moving."

The roadblocks you encounter are not evidence of God's absence—they are a sign of His investment in your future. He is not trying to stop you. He is strengthening you, preparing you, and building endurance for the journey ahead.

"Many are the afflictions of the righteous, but the LORD delivers him out of them all." — **Psalm 34:19 (NKJV)**

"No weapon formed against you shall prosper, and every tongue that rises against you in judgment You shall condemn. This is the heritage of the servants of the LORD, and their righteousness is from Me," says the LORD. — **Isaiah 54:17 (NKJV)**

Roadblocks, when seen through the lens of faith, become revelatory classrooms. They teach you how to fight, who you are, and most importantly, who God is—even when the path ahead seems obstructed.

I. Internal Roadblocks — The Battle Within

Before David ever faced Goliath, he wrestled with internal resistance—fear, doubt, insecurity, and the lingering wounds of rejection. The internal roadblocks we face often roar louder than external enemies because they speak in our own voice.

1. Fear

Fear distorts reality. It magnifies threats and minimizes God's power.

Fear says, "This mountain is bigger than your God."

But faith declares, "My God made this mountain."

Fear paralyzes, but faith propels. Fear magnifies obstacles, but faith magnifies the greatness of God. The battle with fear is often fought within the heart, where it seeks to undermine trust in God's promises. Yet, when we stand firm, faith pushes back.

"For God has not given us a spirit of fear, but of power and of love and of a sound mind." — **2 Timothy 1:7 (NKJV)**

Fear tries to cloud vision, but faith brings clarity. Fear whispers defeat, but faith shouts victory.

Prophetic Declaration — Over Every Roadblock

I decree and declare victory over every roadblock that has stood before you.

No weapon formed against you shall prosper. Every tongue that rises against you in judgment, you shall condemn **(Isaiah 54:17, NKJV).**

I declare that fear is silenced, doubt is dismantled, and discouragement is uprooted.

You are strengthened with might through His Spirit in the inner man (Ephesians 3:16, NKJV).

You shall run and not be weary, you shall walk and not faint **(Isaiah 40:31, NKJV).**

I prophesy clarity in the fog, courage in the conflict, and faith in the fire.

Where the enemy has tried to build barriers, God is establishing bridges.

Where gates have been shut, the Lord is going before you to open double doors,

so that the gates will not be shut (Isaiah 45:2, NKJV).

Every roadblock that once stood in your way is being cleared. Your faith will overcome every internal and external resistance, and you will move forward into the destiny God has set before you.

CHAPTER 5

THE DAMAGE OF ANXIOUSNESS

From **The Pain of Progression** *by Apostle Dr. Robert L. Black (All Scripture: NKJV)*

Anxiety is a thief—a thief of focus, a strangler of faith. It is a subtle saboteur, constantly working behind the scenes to distract and derail destiny. Anxiety is not simply an emotional reaction; it is a spiritual misalignment. It shifts our gaze from the God who controls outcomes to the outcomes we desperately try to control.

Anxiety turns the middle into a maze. It clouds clarity with uncertainty. It shrinks the sovereignty of God and magnifies our own limitations. In the presence of anxiety, we begin to question our identity, and we allow fear to define us rather than the covenant of promise that has already been established over our lives.

Yet, even in the middle of the fog, delay, and noise, the Spirit speaks:

"Peace, be still." **— Mark 4:39**

The same God who rebuked the storm speaks peace to your inner turmoil. Anxiety attempts to pull you under, but in Christ, you are not called to be carried by anxious thoughts. You are called to carry peace through the storm.

"Be anxious for nothing, but in everything by prayer and supplication, with thanksgiving, let your requests be made known to God; and the peace of God, which surpasses all understanding, will guard your hearts and minds through Christ Jesus." — **Philippians 4:6-7**

In moments of anxiety, let prayer be your anchor. Let Thanksgiving reorient your focus. When fear rises, choose to believe that peace has already been spoken over your storm.

Prophetic Declaration — Chapter 5: The Damage of Anxiousness (All Scripture resonance: NKJV)

I decree and declare that anxiety loses its grip on your mind, heart, and destiny.

For God has not given you a spirit of fear, but of power, love, and a sound mind **(2 Timothy 1:7).**

I declare that the peace of God, which surpasses all understanding, will guard your heart and mind through Christ Jesus **(Philippians 4:7).**

Your thoughts come into divine order. Your emotions align with the truth. Your spirit is governed by heaven's authority.

I prophesy that the voice of worry is silenced, and the whisper of faith grows louder.

You cast all your care upon Him, for He cares for you **(1 Peter 5:7).**

Every anxious cycle, sleepless night, and tormenting thought is broken now in Jesus' name.

I declare that you are strengthened with might through His Spirit in your inner man **(Ephesians 3:16).**

Your focus is restored. Your discernment is sharpened. Your hope is renewed.

You will no longer be moved by what you feel; you are anchored in what God has spoken.

I decree a divine exchange over your life:

Beauty for ashes,

The oil of joy for mourning,

The garment of praise for the spirit of heaviness (Isaiah 61:3).

I prophesy that the Lord is your light and your salvation—whom shall you fear?

The Lord is the strength of your life—of whom shall you be afraid? **(Psalm 27:1).**

You will rest. You will recover. You will rise.

I declare that perfect love casts out fear (1 John 4:18).

You abide in His love. You walk in His truth. You stand in His authority.

Your mind is sound. Your heart is steady. Your path is secure in Him.

In Jesus' name, I decree:

Anxiety is broken.

Peace is established.

Faith is fortified.

Purpose is advancing.

Amen.

CHAPTER 6

PURPOSE IS PASSIONATE

From **The Pain of Progression** *by Apostle Dr. Robert L. Black (All Scripture: NKJV)*

Purpose is not passive; it is a living fire. It does not wait for permission to exist—purpose burns with divine conviction because its origin is God. The call of God is not a suggestion; it is a summons. When God places purpose within a believer, passion awakens, and lethargy loses its hold. Passion is not merely emotional excitement; it is spiritual energy powered by divine assignment.

"For zeal for Your house has eaten me up…" — **Psalm 69:9**

"Therefore, I remind you to stir up the gift of God which is in you…" — **2 Timothy 1:6**

Passion is the fuel that carries purpose through the valley, through misunderstanding, through delay, and through the middle. Without passion, purpose can be known but never pursued. With passion, purpose becomes the priority that reorders life according to heaven's agenda.

Pain Awakens Passion

Many discover their passion in the very place they confront their pain. For David, his passion ignited when he heard Goliath mock the armies of the living God. The challenge stirred a holy fire that would not allow him to remain silent. Pain reveals the things we cannot tolerate—whether injustice, bondage, silence, or compromise—and calls us into purpose.

"Who is this uncircumcised Philistine, that he should defy the armies of the living God?" — **1 Samuel 17:26**

Pain is not always punishment; sometimes it is a pointer to purpose. It points you to the battle you were born to fight, the people you were meant to serve, and the territory you were destined to reclaim.

Purpose Will Challenge Your Comfort

Purpose demands movement. Comfort demands maintenance. You cannot keep both. When purpose comes, it stretches your schedules, sanctifies your appetites, corrects your priorities, and calls you out of familiar patterns into faith.

"Arise, shine; For your light has come! And the glory of the LORD is risen upon you." — **Isaiah 60:1**

Comfort can lull you into complacency, but purpose always demands action. Purpose calls you to rise, to shine, to move, and to grow in ways that may feel uncomfortable but lead to divine destiny.

Passion, Purity, and Power

Passion must be stewarded with purity, or it turns into ambition. Passion must be yoked to obedience, or it becomes nothing more than noise. Passion guided by the Spirit becomes power—not human force, but kingdom authority.

"Not by might nor by power, but by My Spirit," says the LORD of hosts. — **Zechariah 4:6**

When passion is consecrated, purpose advances.

When passion is surrendered, power flows.

Purpose fueled by holy passion brings transformation, both in the individual and the world around them. Passion without submission to the Spirit is noise. But passion aligned with God's will becomes the vehicle through which His power flows to accomplish His will on earth.

Reflection Questions — Chapter 6

1. Where has pain revealed the passion of your purpose?
2. What comforts do you need to release in order to obey the assignment God has placed on your life?

3. How will you stir up the gift God has placed within you this week?
4. Where do you sense God's zeal rising in you—and what will you do about it?

Prophetic Activation — Chapter 6

• Write down three places where your holy dissatisfaction burns (injustice, bondage, silence, apathy).

• Pray over each and ask the Spirit for one actionable step to engage your purpose in that area this month.

• Commit to a weekly "altar of zeal"—30 minutes of worship, Word, and strategic planning for your assignment.

Prophetic Prayer — Chapter 6

Father, in Jesus' name, ignite my purpose with holy passion. Burn away complacency, awaken zeal, and align my heart with Your assignment. Sanctify my desires; anchor my obedience, not by might, not by power, but by Your Spirit. Make me a faithful steward of fire—pure, focused, and fruitful. Amen.

Prophetic Declaration — Chapter 6

I decree that purpose burns within you with holy passion. Comfort loses its grip; obedience takes the lead. You are stirred, sanctified, and sent. This is your season to arise and shine, for the glory of the Lord is upon you. In Jesus' name, you will move, you will build, you will fulfill. Amen.

CHAPTER 7

LIVING THE OUTCOME IN FULL VIEW

From **The Pain of Progression** *by Apostle Dr. Robert L. Black (All Scripture: NKJV)*

Progression requires vision, not just movement. Movement without vision is aimless, but vision—divinely inspired vision—anchors our steps in the middle of uncertainty. It is the spiritual preview of the outcome, the picture from God that gives us direction and purpose when our circumstances contradict the promise.

"...God, who gives life to the dead and calls those things which do not exist as though they did." — **Romans 4:17**

"Write the vision and make it plain on tablets, that he may run who reads it." — **Habakkuk 2:2**

Vision is the lens through which we see our future, even while standing in the middle of the process. God often reveals the end from the beginning, so that faith can carry us when our current circumstances tell a different story.

Faith Sees from the Middle

The middle is often noisy. It magnifies obstacles and normalizes delay, distorting our perception of the promise. Vision, however, cuts through the fog and reorders our focus. It says, "I see the outcome, even if I stand in opposition." Vision is not denial; it is an awareness of destiny despite present discomfort.

David carried a vision of kingship long before he ever sat on the throne. The anointing Samuel poured over him was more than an act—it became a living picture, a vision that led him through caves, conflict, and contradiction.

Vision is not about denying the struggle; it is about recognizing that the struggle is shaping you for the outcome.

The Anatomy of Vision

Vision is not merely a wishful thought; it is a divine revelation with a purpose and a process. The anatomy of vision can be broken down into five components:

- **Source:** Vision originates from God. It is not self-imagined but divinely inspired.
- **Substance:** Vision must align with Scripture. It cannot contradict the Word of God; it must be rooted in the truth of His promises.
- **Strategy:** Vision requires steps and stewardship. It is not just a picture; it's a path, a set of actions we must take.

- **Stamina:** Vision requires endurance through opposition. Vision grows stronger the longer we endure.
- **Scale:** Vision grows with obedience. As you take steps in alignment with God's will, the vision expands, and new layers of revelation unfold.

Vision must be written, spoken, guarded, and revisited. Write down the vision God has given you. Rehearse it in your heart and speak it aloud, even when you feel weary. Guard the vision from cynicism, unbelief, and weariness. Revisit it often to keep your soul aligned with God's promise.

"I would have lost heart, unless I had believed that I would see the goodness of the LORD in the land of the living." — **Psalm 27:13**

Progression Demands More Than Movement; It Demands Sight

Progression is not simply about moving forward—it requires prophetic vision. The ability to see the God-ordained outcome while standing in the fog of the middle is critical. Vision is heaven's preview of earth's assignment. It is the picture God places in your spirit so that your steps are governed by revelation, not by the shifting circumstances around you.

The middle is notorious for its noise: delay, contradiction, misunderstanding, and spiritual warfare. These distractions try to blur, shrink, and twist what God has shown you. But vision stands taller than the valley. It speaks when results are silent. It stabilizes faith when emotions tremble.

"Write the vision and make it plain on tablets, that he may run who reads it." — **Habakkuk 2:2**

God "calls those things which do not exist as though they did." — **Romans 4:17**

To live with the outcome in full view is to keep seeing what God has said until what you see aligns with what God has spoken. It is faith wearing sight—the eyes of your spirit fixed on the promise, while your feet continue through the process.

I. Vision: Heaven's Picture, Earth's Path

Vision is not fantasy—it is prophetic strategy. God reveals the end so you can walk the steps. He shows you the crown so you can endure the cave. He unveils the harvest so you can sow with conviction. Vision presents the outcome in full view, so the middle will not master you.

Vision has four companions:

1. **Word:** Vision must agree with Scripture. It cannot contradict the Word of God; it must align with His truth and promises.
2. **Witness:** Vision carries inner confirmation from the Holy Spirit. You will feel an inner peace or affirmation when your vision is in line with God's will.
3. **Wisdom:** Vision requires steps, stewardship, and timing. It is not only about what you see but about how you act on it.
4. **Warfare:** Vision attracts resistance. It challenges the status quo, and this resistance refines your resolve and strengthens your faith.

When Vision Is Seen, It Must Be Written, Spoken, Guarded, and Stewarded

- **Write:** Record the revelation. Name it. Date it. Detail it. This helps solidify the vision in your heart and keeps you focused on the end goal.
- **Speak:** Prophesy the vision aloud. Your words shape your path and bring life to your purpose.
- **Guard:** Protect the vision from cynicism, unbelief, and weariness. Speak life into it when others doubt.
- **Steward:** Turn revelation into routine. Small steps of obedience, consistently taken, will move you closer to the fulfillment of the vision.

II. Examples of Outcome in Full View

David carried the kingship in view long before he wore a crown. The oil Samuel poured on him was not merely an event; it was the installation of vision (1 Samuel 16). David lived the outcome in full view while navigating caves, betrayal, and persecution. The picture of his destiny remained before his eyes, and the middle could not steal it. He carried the promise of kingship even as he endured the valley of opposition.

Abraham lived with the outcome in view as he walked toward a land, a lineage, and a legacy that he could not yet see. God called him out, and Abraham obeyed, sustained by a promise-focused sight (Genesis 12; Romans 4:18–21). Abraham was able to move forward because he saw beyond his current reality into the future God promised.

Joseph saw the outcome in dreams. Though the pit, Potiphar's house, and prison were middle-places, they could not cancel the vision. Joseph stewarded his integrity, excellence, and faith until the outcome found him (Genesis 37–41). His vision of leadership held him steady as he navigated betrayal and hardship.

Nehemiah saw the wall rebuilt before the first stone was lifted. He prayed, planned, asked boldly, fought wisely, and finished quickly—because the picture of the wall's completion governed his pace (Nehemiah 2–6). Nehemiah's ability to see the end goal in full view enabled him to lead with conviction and courage in the midst of adversity.

These are not stories of convenience; they are testimonies of vision that refuse to bow to the middle.

III. The Middle's Fog vs. Heaven's Focus

The middle often carries fog—spiritual haze designed to distort our sight. The fog arrives in the form of:

- **Contradictions:** What you see vs. what God said
- **Delays:** Time stretching beyond expectation
- **Distractions:** Good things diverting you from God's things
- **Doubt:** Internal arguments against divine instruction
- **Disappointment:** Unhealed pain casting shadows on future hope

But fog is not final. Fog can be overcome by the discipline of sight. The fog of the middle does not have to obscure the vision God has given you.

Here are five ways to maintain clarity of sight in the midst of fog:

1. **Revisit the Vision Daily:** Read what you wrote; speak what you saw.
2. **Worship as Warfare:** Praise lifts sight above storms (Psalm 34:3).

3. **Fast for Focus:** Reduce noise to increase clarity (Matthew 6:17–18).

4. **Seek Counsel:** Prophetic and pastoral voices confirm and correct.

5. **Act on Small Steps:** Obedience turns the lights on in the fog.

Your focus is not the middle; your focus is the Master. When He becomes the object of your gaze, the fog becomes a backdrop to His glory.

IV. The Anatomy of a Vision-Bearer

To live the outcome in full view, cultivate vision habits:

- **Sight Over Sentiment:** Emotions are real, but they should not be your guide.

- **Covenant Over Circumstance:** Choose fidelity to the promise over the volatility of situations.

- **Language of Life**: Speak aligned, faith-filled words (Proverbs 18:21).

- **Stewardship of Steps:** Walk in excellence, diligence, and order.

- **Resilience in Warfare:** Expect resistance, but respond with resolve.

Vision-bearers are builders. They do not wait for outcomes; they partner with God to manifest them. They practice prophetic patience—waiting actively, building faithfully, sowing consistently.

"For the vision is yet for an appointed time… Though it tarries, wait for it; because it will surely come." — **Habakkuk 2:3**

The appointed time is not a calendar surprise; it is a character finish line. God times outcomes to match your maturity. The appointed time will come, but it will align with the fullness of your preparation.

V. Holding the End in the Middle

The middle often asks provocative questions: "Did God really say?" "Was that vision real?" "Am I deceived?" Faith answers with Scripture, worship, and prophetic memory. The enemy's goal is to break your connection to the vision. You must refuse to surrender sight.

Three anchors for holding the end in view while standing in the middle:

1. **Memory:** Remember what God has done before (Psalm 77:11).
2. **Meditation:** Keep the Word as your lens (Joshua 1:8).
3. **Momentum:** One obedient step at a time—small steps become great strides.

Vision is kept alive by habitual honor. Honor the vision with your time, thought, talk, and action. Be diligent in nurturing what God has shown you, even when your circumstances seem to contradict the promise.

VI. Practical Strategies for Vision-Stewardship

1. Write a Vision Rule of Life:

Create a weekly structure that ties your vision to daily habits. This may include:

- Prayer (daily)
- Word (daily)
- Worship (daily)
- Fasting (weekly)
- Generosity (monthly)
- Skill development (weekly)
- Mission steps (weekly)

A Vision Rule of Life helps integrate the vision into your everyday actions, turning revelation into routine.

2. Create Vision Milestones:

Break the big outcome into smaller, manageable milestones. Plan by quarters and months, assigning measurable steps and review points. Regularly track progress and hold yourself accountable. The big promise is kept alive by small, consistent steps of obedience.

3. Establish a Prophetic Atmosphere:

Fill your environment with Scriptures, decrees, worship, and testimonies. The atmosphere around you sustains the vision within you. What surrounds you will start to form you, so create an environment that nurtures your faith, aligns with your vision, and supports your progress.

4. Recruit Vision Allies:

Invite intercessors, mentors, and trusted voices into your journey. Ask them to pray, review, and encourage you. Isolation weakens vision, but community strengthens it. A group of people aligned with your purpose can help clarify your focus and lift your spirit when obstacles arise.

5. Guard Against Vision Vandals:

Limit access to voices that minimize faith, mock your dreams, or magnify fear. Love all, but steward your access wisely. Not everyone has the vision for your future, so protect your spirit by wisely choosing who speaks into your life.

VII. Living the Outcome in Your Language

Your language must align with your outcome. What you say will eventually shape what you see. Speak the promises of God over your life until what you speak becomes what you see.

- **Present Tense of Promise:** Speak in the present tense as though the promise is already in motion:
  - "I am building."
  - "I am becoming."
  - "I am advancing."
- **Covenant Language:** Use language that affirms God's presence and favor:
  - "God is with me."
  - "Favor surrounds me."
  - "Grace empowers me."
- **Outcome Decrees:** Declare the future as though it's already assured:
  - "I will see it."
  - "I will finish."
  - "I will fulfill."

Words are not merely sentences; they are spiritual scaffolding. They hold up your vision and support the structure of your destiny as it is being erected.

VIII. When the Vision Feels Distant

If you feel distant from the outcome, do not despair— draw near. The feeling of distance is not permanent; it is a signal to pursue God's presence even more deeply. When the vision seems far off, it's time to press in. Draw near to God, to His Word, and to the altar.

"I would have lost heart, unless I had believed that I would see the goodness of the LORD in the land of the living." — **Psalm 27:13**

Distance may feel discouraging, but it is often a moment that beckons you to lean into God even more. Keep your eyes on the outcome, and trust that He is working, even when it feels like you are waiting.

In these final moments, remember: the middle is not permanent. The journey toward the fulfillment of your vision is a process, but it's a process that is leading you somewhere. Hold the outcome in full view, speak it into existence, and keep moving forward with divine conviction. The Lord is with you every step of the way.

CHAPTER 8

P.A.I.N. — Positional, Agreement, Identifying, Normalcy

From **The Pain of Progression** *by Apostle Dr. Robert L. Black (All Scripture: NKJV)*

Pain is not merely something you endure; it is something you encounter with purpose. It is not only what happens to you—it is what God shapes within you through the experience. In the kingdom, pain is rarely punitive; it is often preparative. The middle becomes a refining furnace where pressure produces strength and stretching produces stability.

The acronym **P.A.I.N.** reveals four dimensions through which the Spirit develops believers during seasons of tension:

- **P — Positional**
- **A — Agreement**
- **I — Identifying**
- **N — Normalcy**

Each dimension reframes pain as purposeful progression. The middle is not evidence of being lost—it is evidence of alignment.

"My brethren, count it all joy when you fall into various trials…" — James 1:2

<u>P — Positional</u>

Pain positions you for purpose. God often uses uncomfortable placement to align you with His timing, training, and testimony. What feels like displacement is frequently divine positioning.

Biblical Examples

David (1 Samuel 16:13; Psalm 23:1–4)

David was anointed in his father's house but sent back to the pasture. What appeared to be a demotion was actually development. The field formed a warrior; the valley revealed a king.

Insight: Your current place may feel beneath your calling, but it is building the capacity your calling will require.

Joseph (Genesis 37–50)

Joseph moved from the pit to Potiphar's house to prison before reaching the palace. Each stage appeared unjust, yet each placement was purposeful.

Key verse: "You meant evil against me; but God meant it for good…" (Genesis 50:20).

Insight: Strategic positioning often arrives disguised as a setback.

Esther (Esther 2–4)

Esther was positioned as queen not for luxury, but for leverage—"for such a time as this" (Esther 4:14).

Insight: Favor is placement for assignment, not applause.

Modern **and** Ministry **Applications**

- **Marketplace Positioning:** A lateral move, reassignment, or unexpected transition may expose you to relationships, skill development, or visibility necessary for future advancement.

- **Church Positioning:** Serving behind the scenes—intercession, administration, logistics—may feel hidden, yet it cultivates precision, humility, and trustworthiness.

Positioning is rarely glamorous, but it is always strategic.

Simple Activation — Positional

- Map your middle: Write down where God currently has you—home, work, church. Under each category, identify one way this placement is strengthening your character, skills, or faith.

- Decree: "I am not stuck; I am strategically placed."

A — Agreement

Pain invites agreement with God's process. We do not merely agree with outcomes; we agree with the path that produces them. True alignment is not just celebrating fulfillment—it is consenting to formation.

Biblical Examples

Mary (Luke 1:38)

"Behold the maidservant of the Lord! Let it be to me according to your word."

Mary's agreement made room for incarnation.

Insight: Agreement is the gateway through which promise becomes reality.

Jesus (Luke 22:42)

"Nevertheless, not My will, but Yours, be done." In Gethsemane, anguish became alignment.

Insight: Agreement transforms suffering into stewardship.

Abraham (Romans 4:20–21)

He "did not waver at the promise of God through unbelief," remaining fully convinced.

Insight: Agreement is sustained conviction during prolonged delay.

Agreement does not remove discomfort; it redeems it. It anchors the heart when circumstances stretch beyond explanation.

Modern **and** Ministry **Applications**

- **Healing and Wholeness:** Choosing counseling or inner healing—though uncomfortable—can become the doorway to freedom and greater capacity for leadership.

- **Financial Alignment:** Practicing generosity when resources feel tight reflects agreement that God's economy governs your increase.

- **Leadership Formation:** Submitting to mentorship, correction, and pruning affirms that growth requires refinement (John 15:2).

Agreement is not passive resignation; it is active surrender.

Simple Activation — Agreement

- Write a "Let It Be" prayer. Identify the process you have resisted and surrender it intentionally, line by line.

- Decree:

  "I agree with God's way, God's timing, and God's training."

I — Identifying

Pain clarifies identity and exposes opposition—both internal and external. Identification is discernment. It distinguishes what strengthens your purpose from what weakens it. It reveals where boundaries are necessary and where alignment must deepen.

Biblical Examples

David and Goliath (1 Samuel 17:26)

"Who is this uncircumcised Philistine…?" David identified both the enemy's lack of covenant and his own covenant advantage.

Insight: Name the true battle and remember your spiritual authority.

Nehemiah (Nehemiah 4–6)

Sanballat and Tobiah represented distraction, intimidation, and slander.

Insight: Some voices exist to halt building; discernment keeps you on the wall.

Paul (Acts 16:16–18)

He discerned a spirit of divination—what sounded supportive was spiritual sabotage.

Insight: Not every affirmation is in alignment.

Discernment protects destiny.

Internal Identification — Soul Inventory

- **Patterns:** Where do perfectionism, procrastination, or people-pleasing undermine obedience?

- **Triggers:** What situations—rejection, comparison, scarcity—destabilize focus?

- **Allies:** Who consistently speaks truth, faith, and correction into your life?

Self-awareness strengthens spiritual authority.

Modern and Ministry Applications

- **Digital Discernment:** Limit voices that amplify fear or cynicism. Increase exposure to voices anchored in Scripture and vision.

- **Boundary Setting:** Reduce access to relationships that dilute focus; strengthen connection with those who sharpen faith.

Discernment Tools (NKJV Lens)

- **Scripture Test:** Does it align with the Word? (2 Timothy 3:16–17)

- **Fruit Test:** Does it produce love, joy, peace, and self-control? (Galatians 5:22–23)

- **Peace Witness:** Does the peace of God rule in your heart? (Colossians 3:15)

Discernment ensures that pain refines rather than derails.

Simple Activation — Identifying

- Make two lists: What fuels your purpose (people, places, practices) and what frays it. Adjust your rhythms accordingly.

- Decree: "I identify and reject what hinders; I embrace what advances."

<u>N — Normalcy</u>

Pain matures you until obedience becomes normal. Normalcy is not spiritual boredom—it is spiritual stability. It is when discipline becomes delight and maturity becomes routine. Holy habits form a framework that sustains progression and stabilizes sight.

Biblical Examples

Daniel (Daniel 6:10)

"As was his custom," he prayed three times a day—even under threat.

Insight: Customized devotion creates unshakable consistency.

Jesus (Luke 4:16; 5:16)

He had a custom of synagogue engagement and often withdrew to pray.

Insight: Rhythm produces resilience.

The Early Church (Acts 2:42)

They continued steadfastly in doctrine, fellowship, breaking bread, and prayers.

Insight: Community rhythms build durable faith.

Normalcy is what keeps faith steady when emotion fluctuates. It is the quiet strength of repeated obedience.

Modern **and** Ministry **Applications**

Rule of Life: Daily Word and prayer, weekly fasting, consistent generosity, monthly solitude or retreat, and scheduled accountability.

- **Sabbath Practice:** A 24-hour rhythm of rest to reset clarity, joy, and creativity.

- **Skill Stewardship:** Regular investment into the craft connected to your assignment—leadership, preaching, administration, writing, or service.

Maturity becomes visible when obedience is no longer seasonal but sustained.

Simple Activation — Normalcy

- Design your "Holy Routine": Choose three daily habits (Word, prayer, worship), two weekly habits (fasting, service), and one monthly habit (solitude or retreat). Schedule them intentionally.

- Decree: "Maturity is my new normal; consistency is my culture."

Putting P.A.I.N. Together — A Flow Example

Scenario: You feel "stuck" in a role beneath your gifting.

1. **Positional:** Recognize that God has placed you strategically to learn systems, stewardship, and humility—like David in the field.

2. **Agreement:** Pray, "Let it be to me…" and serve with excellence, following the examples of Mary and Jesus in surrender.

3. **Identifying:** Discern internal discouragement and external distractions. Strengthen wise allies, as Nehemiah did, and practice discernment like Paul.

4. **Normalcy:** Establish consistent rhythms, as seen in Daniel and the early church, until faithfulness becomes your default and promotion aligns with maturity.

Pain is not random—it is revelatory. When understood through P.A.I.N., the middle becomes a classroom instead of a cage.

Short Prophetic Decree Over P.A.I.N.

I decree that your positioning is purposeful, your agreement unlocks advancement, your identification clarifies your path, and maturity becomes your norm.

In Jesus' name, you are being formed for fulfillment. Amen.

CHAPTER 9

FAILURE IS NEVER AN OPTION WHEN FAITH EMBRACES PROGRESSION

From **The Pain of Progression** *by Apostle Dr. Robert L. Black (All Scripture: NKJV)*

Failure is the word the enemy uses to rename your process; faith is the word God uses to define your victory. In the kingdom, failure is not a final outcome—it is a decision to stop moving. As long as faith endures, failure loses authority. When progression is embraced, setbacks become classrooms, delays become development, and weakness becomes the altar where strength is formed.

"Being confident of this very thing, that He who has begun a good work in you will complete it until the day of Jesus Christ." — Philippians 1:6

"For a righteous man may fall seven times and rise again, but the wicked shall fall by calamity." — Proverbs 24:16

Faith is not fragile optimism; it is covenant conviction rooted in the unchanging character of God. Faith does not deny pain—it declares purpose within it. Faith does not silence opposition—it outlasts it. Faith keeps you standing in seasons designed to scatter you.

I. The Myth of Failure in God

For the believer who embraces progression, failure is a distortion—not a destiny. The only true failure in God's economy is refusing to continue. If you keep believing, keep obeying, keep repenting, keep learning, keep worshiping, keep showing up—you cannot fail.

You may be refined.

You may be redirected.

You may be repaired.

But you will not be ruined.

"And we know that all things work together for good to those who love God, to those who are called according to His purpose." — Romans 8:28

The middle often mislabels seasons. What you called loss, God called a lesson. What you named defeat, God identified as development. What felt like an ending, heaven recorded as editing.

Faith declares: "I am still in His hands."

Progression affirms: "I am still in His plan."

Grace reminds: "I am still in His story."

II. The Witnesses of Progression: David, Peter, Joseph

David stumbled, yet he did not fail. His life reflects the tension of anointing and humanity—victories intertwined with vulnerability. When he fell, he repented. When he erred, he returned. His restoration did not erase consequence, but it reaffirmed the covenant.

"Create in me a clean heart, O God, and renew a steadfast spirit within me." — Psalm 51:10

Repentance preserved his purpose. His failure was not final because his faith remained responsive.

Peter denied Jesus, but denial did not define him. Christ prayed that Peter's faith would not fail (Luke 22:32), and later restored him with recommissioning: "Feed My sheep" (John 21:17). The same mouth that denied became the voice that declared at Pentecost. The stumble became the scar that softened his shepherding.

Joseph was betrayed, sold, falsely accused, and forgotten—yet not failed. Each unjust season became infrastructure for righteous leadership. The pit trained humility. The prison cultivated integrity. The palace revealed stewardship. What looked like a loss was laying the foundation.

Their lives testify to a consistent truth: a believer who keeps moving cannot be mastered by failure.

III. Progression Converts Setbacks into Strength

Progression is not merely forward movement; it is forward formation. God forms you through what confronts you. He turns wounds into wisdom, pressure into persistence, and disappointment into discernment.

- **Setbacks** become signal posts—revealing areas God intends to strengthen.

- **Delays** become detox—purifying motives and refining desires.

- **Closed doors** become course corrections— shielding you from premature exposure.

- **Criticism** becomes calibration—sharpening excellence and strengthening authority.

"My brethren, count it all joy when you fall into various trials, knowing that the testing of your faith produces patience." — James 1:2–3

Testing is not termination; it is transformation. Trials are not verdicts; they are tools. What appears to oppose you may be preparing you. Progression reframes every setback as a strength under construction.

CHAPTER 10

THE RESTORATION IN THE VALLEY

From **The Pain of Progression** *by Apostle Dr. Robert L. Black (All Scripture: NKJV)*

The valley is not your burial ground—it is your birthplace. In the kingdom of God, restoration is not a return to former strength; it is the unveiling of a greater version of who you were always meant to become. Every valley carries a voice, and every valley carries an assignment. Valleys are not evidence of God's absence; they are arenas of divine reconstruction.

Restoration is rarely birthed on mountaintops. It unfolds in low places—where pride is dismantled, vision sharpens, humility deepens, and faith matures. The valley is where you are stripped, shaped, and strengthened simultaneously.

"He restores my soul; He leads me in the paths of righteousness. For His name's sake." — Psalm 23:3 (NKJV)

Restoration is not mere repair. It is re-creation. God does not simply piece broken fragments back together; He forms new strength that could not have existed without the breaking. Where there was loss, He restores with increase.

Where suffering cuts deeply, redemption reaches further. Where darkness lingered, light now floods.

The valley is often the place where God completes what He began.

I. The Valley Is a Refining Place Before a Restoring Place

Many believers misinterpret the valley as abandonment when it is actually an appointment. Throughout Scripture, the valley is where:

- Identity is revealed
- Calling is tested
- Trust is proven
- Obedience is purified
- Character is forged

The valley refines before it restores.

David's Valley of Refining

David did not become king in the palace—he became king in the valley.

It was in caves, wilderness seasons, and hidden places where dependence on God replaced dependence on self. In obscurity, his leadership matured. In isolation, his intimacy deepened.

He learned:

- How to worship without crowds

- How to war without applause

- How to pray without platforms

- How to seek God without safety

The valley stripped away the counterfeit and strengthened the authentic.

"It was good for me that I have been afflicted, That I may learn Your statutes." — Psalm 119:71 (NKJV)

Affliction became education. Hardship became training. The valley became the classroom that crowned him long before Israel ever did.

Restoration begins with refinement.

II. Restoration Has a Divine Order

Biblical restoration follows a prophetic sequence. God does not rebuild randomly; He restores intentionally and in order.

1. God Restores Your Soul

Before He restores opportunities, He restores identity.

Before He restores platforms, He restores purity.

Before He restores relationships, He restores your spiritual rhythm.

"He restores my soul." — Psalm 23:3

The soul is often the primary battleground in the valley. It absorbs:

- Exhaustion

- Confusion

- Anxiety

- Shame

- Grief

- Inner fragmentation

The Shepherd touches the soul first because unresolved internal wounds can sabotage external breakthroughs. Restoration begins within. When the soul is stabilized, the structure can be strengthened.

God repairs what is unseen before He elevates what is visible.

2. God Restores Your Sight

You cannot walk confidently into what you cannot see clearly.

Many lose vision in the valley. That loss is not punishment—it is preparation for a clearer lens. God often removes former perspectives to install refined perception.

He restores:

- Prophetic clarity

- Direction

- Discernment

- Spiritual sensitivity

Before elevation comes illumination. Before movement comes revelation, sight restored means confusion loses authority.

3. God Restores Your Steps

Once the soul and sight are aligned, movement is restored.

"He leads me in the paths of righteousness for His name's sake." — Psalm 23:3

He orders your:

- Decisions

- Timing

- Partnerships

- Assignments

Your pace becomes synchronized with heaven's rhythm. You no longer move from anxiety but from authority. You no longer act from panic but from purpose.

Restored steps reflect restored trust.

4. God Restores Your Strength

The valley drains human strength. Restoration replaces it with divine endurance.

"But those who wait on the LORD shall renew their strength…" — Isaiah 40:31

Renewal is not simple recovery—it is exchange. You surrender depleted strength and receive sustained endurance.

You emerge from the valley:

- Stronger
- Wiser
- Sharper
- More resilient
- More rooted in God

What once exhausted you now equips you.

5. God Restores Your Seat (Position and Influence)

After refining, rebuilding, and renewing—God repositions you.

Not where you were.

Beyond where you were.

Like David:

- You are seated differently

- You operate differently

- You carry authority differently

- You seek God differently

Restoration prepares you for greater stewardship. It is not the end of the process—it is the doorway to promotion.

III. The Valley Is Often God's Last Work Before Elevation

The valley is frequently God's finishing place. Before He launches you, He perfects you. Before He reveals you, He refines you. Before He multiplies you, He matures you.

Scripture consistently reveals this pattern:

Joseph

Restoration after betrayal led to exaltation as prime minister. The pit and prison prepared him for governance.

Job

Restoration followed suffering—and it was multiplied.

"The LORD blessed the latter days of Job more than his beginning." — Job 42:12

Peter

Restoration followed failure and led to apostolic commissioning. His denial did not disqualify him; restoration repositioned him.

Israel

Restoration after wilderness wandering preceded inheritance in the promised land.

And you—Restoration in the middle becomes progression into purpose.

The valley is not a detour. It is often the final preparation before elevation.

IV. Restoration Requires Surrender

You cannot resist God's refining and receive His restoring at the same time. Restoration begins where surrender becomes sincere.

Surrender prays:

"Lord, do in me what I cannot do."

"Lord, heal what I cannot reach."

"Lord, rebuild what I cannot carry."

"Lord, correct what I cannot see."

Restoration flows through yielded vessels, not striving ones. God restores what we release into His hands.

V. Signs That Restoration Has Begun

Restoration does not always arrive with noise. It often begins quietly and steadily. You may notice:

1. Your peace returning

2. Your appetite for God increasing

3. Your joy becoming internal rather than situational

4. Your discernment sharpening

5. Your voice regaining confidence

6. You no longer mourning what was lost

7. New dreams forming

8. Strength rising without effort

9. Forgiveness flowing more freely

10. Progression resuming naturally

When restoration begins, it carries a quiet assurance. The Spirit whispers, "You're ready."

Reflection Questions — Chapter 10

1. Where have you sensed God refining you in the valley?

2. Which area needs restoration first—your soul, sight, strength, or steps?

3. What signs of restoration have already begun to surface?

4. What must you surrender to deepen God's restoring work?

5. Who are you becoming because of the valley?

Prophetic Activation — Chapter 10

1. **Write your "Restoration Map:"**

   Divide a page into four sections: Soul, Sight, Steps, Strength.

   List what God is restoring in each area.

2. **Prophetic Worship Session:**

   Play worship that stirs restoration—psalms, psalters, or string-instrument worship.

   Invite the Holy Spirit to highlight your next step forward.

3. **Speak Out Loud:**

   "My valley is becoming my launching pad."

Prophetic Prayer — Chapter 10

Father, restore me in the deep places of my soul. Restore clarity to my sight, courage to my heart, and order to my steps. Renew my strength like the eagle.

Heal the places of brokenness, rebuild the foundations of my faith, and reignite the fire of my purpose. I surrender to Your process. Lead me through the valley and establish me on the mountain You have prepared for me.

In Jesus' name, amen.

Prophetic Declaration — Chapter 10: The Restoration in the Valley

I decree and declare that your valley is becoming your victory. You are being restored in your soul, your sight, your strength, and your steps.

The hand of the Lord is upon you to rebuild, revive, and restore.

Every wound is being healed.

Every weakness is being strengthened.

Every delay is being redeemed.

Every broken piece is becoming a masterpiece.

The season of heaviness lifts now.

The mantle of restoration rests upon you.

You are rising in kingdom identity, walking in renewed authority, and moving in divine clarity.

In Jesus' name:

You will not die in the valley.

You will be restored in the valley.

And you will be promoted from the valley.

Amen.

Conclusion — Purpose Prevails

Progression was never meant to be painless—only purposeful. Throughout this journey, you have walked through valleys, navigated transitions, and learned to reinterpret the middle not as punishment, but as preparation. The places you least preferred became the spaces where God worked most deeply. What stretched you also strengthened you. What humbled you also healed you. What frustrated you also formed you.

The middle refined your faith. It clarified your identity. It revealed a strength you did not know you possessed.

Spiritual maturity is not measured by how loudly we worship on the mountain, but by how faithfully we trust in the valley. It is the decision to believe when feelings fluctuate, to obey when instructions are uncomfortable, and to stand when life shakes what once felt stable. The middle cultivated resilience. It deepened surrender. It strengthened dependence.

And now, a breakthrough stands before you.

Not because the process was easy—but because the process was ordained. Progression was unfolding even when it felt hidden. Breakthrough was forming even when you felt fractured. Every tear watered growth. Every delay developed depth. Every disappointment laid the foundation.

You have outgrown who you were. You are stepping into who God has called you to become.

This is your prophetic push:

You will not go back.

You will not break down.

You will not lose what God built in you through pain.

You are advancing.

You are maturing.

You are progressing—intentionally and purposefully.

Let this truth echo long after these pages are closed: God never wastes pain. Not a season. Not a tear. Not a moment. He redeems, restores, reshapes, and repurposes every part of the journey. What felt like breaking was building. What felt like a delay was alignment. What felt like loss was preparation for glory.

You are living proof that pain can propel promise. You are evidence that the middle was not the end. You are testimony that progression—though painful—leads to destiny.

Walk boldly into your next chapter.

Purpose has prevailed.

And so have you.

THE PAIN OF PROGRESSION — SELF ASSESSMENT WORKBOOK

Reflect. Realign. Rise.

This workbook is designed to help you evaluate where you are, what God is revealing, and how you are being shaped "in the middle." Work through these questions slowly, prayerfully, and honestly. Your answers are part of your progression.

SECTION 1 — Understanding Your Middle

1. Where Are You Right Now?

Use the prompts below to identify your current "middle" season:

- What feels uncomfortable right now?

- What feels stagnant, delayed, or uncertain?

- What areas of your life feel like a valley— emotionally, spiritually, or mentally?

Reflection:

- In what ways does your current season remind you of David's valley experience?

- What "lions and bears" are you being trained to defeat?

Journal Space:

Write freely here…

SECTION 2 — Purpose vs. Process

2. Are You Confusing Process with Purpose?

- What steps or plans have you been focusing on more than God's "why" for your life?

- Have you become more loyal to the instructions than to the vision behind them?

- What processes are structured but no longer Spirit-led?

Scripture Reflection:

Romans 8:28 reminds us that **"we know"**—through experience—that God works *all* things for good.

- What have you "come to know" about God through your middle season?

- Where has pain taught you something that process never could?

SECTION 3 — Identifying the Pain That Is Producing You

3. What Pain Is Preparing You?

Affliction carries goodness through God's lens (Psalm 119:71).

Reflect on the following:

- What recent struggle taught you a lesson you could not have learned any other way?

- What emotional or spiritual muscles are being strengthened through discomfort?

- What did the middle expose in you—fear, pride, insecurity, doubt—that God is now healing?

Assessment Scale (1–5): Rate your agreement with the statements below:

Statement	1	2	3	4	5
I recognize that pain has a purpose in my life.	☐	☐	☐	☐	☐
I sense God maturing me in this season.	☐	☐	☐	☐	☐
I trust God even when I don't understand the process.	☐	☐	☐	☐	☐
I believe this middle season is producing long-term fruit.	☐	☐	☐	☐	☐

SECTION 4 — The David Assessment: Strength in the Valley

4. The Vast Valley Evaluation

David's middle taught him three things: **Identity. Discernment. Confidence in God.**

Reflect on these same areas:

Identity Check:

- How has the middle clarified *who you are*?

- What labels has God removed from you—failure, unqualified, overlooked, unworthy?

Discernment Check:

- Who or what are the "Goliaths" standing against your progression?

- What battles are not yours to fight?

- Which battles is God empowering you to win?

Confidence Check:

Finish this statement:

"Because God is with me, I will defeat…"

SECTION 5 — Christ in the Middle

5. The Jesus Reflection

Jesus endured His middle at Calvary—yet He stayed anchored in purpose.

- What parts of your current journey feel like crucifixion (dying to self, surrendering plans, releasing old identities)?

- Where is God inviting you to embrace obedience over comfort?

- What is God resurrecting in your life as a result of your endurance?

Prayer Prompt:

"Lord, give me the courage to endure my middle with the same purpose-driven resolve Jesus modeled."

SECTION 6 — Your Progression Map

6. What Is God Forming in You?

Complete the progression steps below:

I am being processed in the area of:

- **God is maturing me by teaching me to:**

- **The middle is preparing me to walk in:**

- **God is revealing this new identity in me:**

- **I sense God removing:**

- **I sense God strengthening:**

- **I sense God calling me toward:**

SECTION 7 — Prophetic Declaration Over Your Journey

Speak this over your life:

I declare that I am not stuck—I am being shaped.

I am not failing—I am being fortified.

I am not overlooked—I am being developed.

Every valley is training me for victory.

Every delay is aligning me with destiny.

Every battle is preparing me for a breakthrough.

My pain has purpose, and my purpose will prevail.

God is with me in the middle.

And because of that, I cannot be defeated."

SECTION 8 — Final Self-Assessment: Are You Progressing?

Answer Yes or No

1. Am I growing in spiritual maturity during this season?

2. Am I learning to trust God beyond my understanding?

3. Am I recognizing the purpose behind my pain?

4. Am I becoming more aligned with God's identity for me?

5. Am I responding to challenges with faith instead of fear?

6. Am I becoming more stable, balanced, and strengthened in the middle?

7. Am I allowing God to transform me rather than resisting the process?

If you answered "Yes" to 4 or more, you are progressing—even if it doesn't feel like it.

SECTION 9 — Closing Reflection

Write a final reflection based on your journey through this workbook:

- What have you learned about yourself?

- What have you learned about God?

- What is the one truth from this book you will carry forward?

- What commitment are you making as you move from the middle into maturity?

30-Day Progression Devotional

Becoming Who God Saw from the Beginning

DAY 1 — The Middle Has Meaning

Scripture: Romans 8:28

Focus: You are not stuck; you are being shaped.

Reflection: Where do you feel "in the middle"? What might God be forming there?

Declaration: *Everything in my life is working together for good.*

Prayer: *Lord, help me see the purpose behind my process.*

DAY 2 — When Promise Meets Pain

Scripture: Psalm 34:19

Reflection: Pain is not divine punishment—it's divine preparation.

Declaration: *Every affliction is equipping me.*

Prayer: *Give me courage when progression hurts.*

DAY 3 — David's Valley Lessons

Scripture: 1 Samuel 17:37

Reflection: What lions and bears are preparing you for Goliath?

Declaration: *My history with God gives me confidence today.*

Prayer: *Help me remember Your faithfulness.*

DAY 4 — God Is With You in the Middle

Scripture: Joshua 1:9

Reflection: In what areas have you felt alone?

Declaration: *I am never abandoned in the process.*

Prayer: *Make Your presence real in my middle.*

DAY 5 — Purpose Over Comfort

Scripture: Matthew 16:24

Reflection: What comfort must you give up to grow?

Declaration: *I choose calling over comfort.*

Prayer: *Strengthen my willingness to surrender.*

DAY 6 — The Beauty of Becoming

Scripture: Philippians 1:6

Reflection: Who are you becoming through your valley?

Declaration: *God is completing what He started in me.*

Prayer: *Continue Your work in my heart.*

DAY 7 — Clarity in the Chaos

Scripture: Psalm 32:8

Reflection: Where do you need direction?

Declaration: *God is guiding me step by step.*

Prayer: *Illuminate my next step.*

DAY 8 — Purpose Requires Pruning

Scripture: John 15:2

Reflection: What is God cutting off in this season?

Declaration: *Pruning is making me more fruitful.*

Prayer: *Remove what no longer belongs.*

DAY 9 — The Weight of Waiting

Scripture: Isaiah 40:31

Reflection: What is waiting producing in you?

Declaration: *My waiting is working.*

Prayer: *Renew my strength as I wait.*

DAY 10 — Identity Revealed in Process

Scripture: 1 Peter 2:9

Reflection: What false identities is God breaking?

Declaration: *I am chosen and called.*

Prayer: *Reveal the truth of who I am.*

DAY 11 — Strength for the Stretch

Scripture: Isaiah 54:2

Reflection: Where is God stretching you?

Declaration: *The stretch is expanding my capacity.*

Prayer: *Help me endure the stretch.*

DAY 12 — Peace in Progression

Scripture: Philippians 4:7

Reflection: Where do you need peace today?

Declaration: *The peace of God anchors me.*

Prayer: *Guard my heart and mind.*

DAY 13 — Valuing the Valley

Scripture: Psalm 23:4

Reflection: What valley has brought unexpected lessons?

Declaration: *I fear no valley with God beside me.*

Prayer: *Walk with me in every dark place.*

DAY 14 — Endurance Births Greatness

Scripture: James 1:2–4

Reflection: How is God using endurance to mature you?

Declaration: *I am being made complete.*

Prayer: *Perfect my endurance.*

DAY 15 — The Ministry of Affliction

Scripture: Psalm 119:71

Reflection: What did recent affliction teach you?

Declaration: *Affliction is my teacher, not my enemy.*

Prayer: *Give me perspective in my pain.*

DAY 16 —Healing Through Humility

Scripture: James 4:10

Reflection: Where is God calling you to humility?

Declaration: *God lifts me as I humble myself.*

Prayer: *Strip away pride and self-reliance.*

DAY 17 — Trusting Beyond Logic

Scripture: Proverbs 3:5–6

Reflection: What are you trying too hard to understand?

Declaration: *I trust God more than my understanding.*

Prayer: *Lead me in Your wisdom.*

DAY 18 — Learning Obedience in the Middle

Scripture: Hebrews 5:8

Reflection: What obedience is God requiring now?

Declaration: *Obedience is building my purpose.*

Prayer: *Give me grace to obey quickly.*

DAY 19 — Strengthened by the Spirit

Scripture: Ephesians 3:16

Reflection: Where do you feel weak?

Declaration: *God strengthens my inner man.*

Prayer: *Fill me with supernatural strength.*

DAY 20 — Confidence in the Calling

Scripture: Psalm 27:3

Reflection: What is challenging your confidence?

Declaration: *I am bold because God is with me.*

Prayer: *Make me confident in Your calling.*

DAY 21 — Stability in Transition

Scripture: Psalm 16:8

Reflection: What transition feels unstable?

Declaration: *I will not be moved.*

Prayer: *Fix my eyes on You.*

DAY 22 — Becoming Battle Ready

Scripture: Ephesians 6:11

Reflection: Where is the enemy attacking in this season?

Declaration: *I stand firm in God's armor.*

Prayer: *Strengthen me for spiritual battle.*

DAY 23 — Protected in the Process

Scripture: Isaiah 43:2

Reflection: Where has God protected you?

Declaration: *I am covered in every season.*

Prayer: *Thank You for being my refuge.*

DAY 24 — Sharpened by Struggle

Scripture: 1 Peter 5:10

Reflection: How is God restoring and establishing you?

Declaration: *Struggle strengthens me.*

Prayer: *Make me firm and steadfast.*

DAY 25 — God's Purpose Prevails

Scripture: Proverbs 19:21

Reflection: What plans did God override for your good?

Declaration: *Purpose is prevailing over my plans.*

Prayer: *Align my desires with Your purpose.*

DAY 26 — Glory After This

Scripture: 2 Corinthians 4:17

Reflection: What eternal weight is God producing in you?

Declaration: *My pain is producing glory.*

Prayer: *Help me see beyond temporary suffering.*

DAY 27 — Strength in Surrender

Scripture: Matthew 26:39

Reflection: What must you surrender for progression?

Declaration: *Not my will, but Yours.*

Prayer: *Teach me the power of surrender.*

DAY 28 — Becoming Who God Saw

Scripture: Jeremiah 1:5

Reflection: Who is God calling you to rise into?

Declaration: *I am becoming the person God designed.*

Prayer: *Reveal Your original intent for me.*

DAY 29 — Crossing into Completion

Scripture: 2 Timothy 4:7

Reflection: What have you finished in this season?

Declaration: *I will finish strong.*

Prayer: *Help me run well and finish well.*

DAY 30 — Purpose Has Prevailed

Scripture: Romans 8:37

Reflection: What victories can you already see?

Declaration: *I am more than a conqueror.*

Prayer: *Thank You for carrying me from pain to progression.*